Samuel French Acting Edition

If You Can Get to Buffalo

An Exploration of Julian Dibbell's "A Rape in Cyberspace"

by Trish Harnetiaux

SAMUELFRENCH.COM   SAMUELFRENCH.CO.UK

ISBN 978-0-573-70580-9

www.SamuelFrench.com
www.SamuelFrench.co.uk

FOR PRODUCTION ENQUIRIES

UNITED STATES AND CANADA
Info@SamuelFrench.com
1-866-598-8449

UNITED KINGDOM AND EUROPE
Plays@SamuelFrench.co.uk
020-7255-4302

Each title is subject to availability from Samuel French, depending upon country of performance. Please be aware that *IF YOU CAN GET TO BUFFALO* may not be licensed by Samuel French in your territory. Professional and amateur producers should contact the nearest Samuel French office or licensing partner to verify availability.

MUSIC USE NOTE

Licensees are solely responsible for obtaining formal written permission from copyright owners to use copyrighted music in the performance of this play and are strongly cautioned to do so. If no such permission is obtained by the licensee, then the licensee must use only original music that the licensee owns and controls. Licensees are solely responsible and liable for all music clearances and shall indemnify the copyright owners of the play(s) and their licensing agent, Samuel French, against any costs, expenses, losses and liabilities arising from the use of music by licensees. Please contact the appropriate music licensing authority in your territory for the rights to any incidental music.

IMPORTANT BILLING AND CREDIT REQUIREMENTS

If you have obtained performance rights to this title, please refer to your licensing agreement for important billing and credit requirements.

IF YOU CAN GET TO BUFFALO was first produced by the Acme Corporation (Lola B. Pierson, Co-Artistic Director; Stephen Nunns, Co-Artistic Director) at St. Mark's Lutheran Church in Baltimore, Maryland on May 16, 2013. The performance was directed by Eric Nightengale, with production design by Eric Nightengale and projection design by Jacob A. Ware. The production stage manager was Janice Rattigan. The cast was as follows:

"STARSINGER" .... Maddie Hicks

"LEGBA" / "GRENDLEFISH" / "BILL GATES" / WIFE .... Katelin McMullin

"JUNIPER" / JOHN (FROM THE NEW YORKER) / "BAMBI" .... Stephen Nunns

"DR. BOMBAY" / JULIAN .... Jesse Marciniak

CHUCK PETAL .... Mike Smith

"MR. BUNGLE" / MAN / "LEGBA (MALE)" .... Daniel Douek

IF YOU CAN GET TO BUFFALO was subsequently produced at the Incubator Arts Project (Samara Naeymi, Producing Director) at St. Mark's Church in New York, New York on February 13, 2014. The play was produced in association with Allison Lyman's company Teeth of Tooth Atelier. The performance was directed by Eric Nightengale, with production design by Eric Nightengale, sound design by Rob Erickson, costume design by Caitlin Conci, and projection design by Jacob A. Ware. The production stage manager was Yaman Palak. The cast was as follows:

"STARSINGER" .... Julia Sirna-Frest

"LEGBA" .... Alex Viola

"GRENDLEFISH" / "PURPLE GUEST" / WIFE / "BILL GATES" .... Minna Taylor

"JUNIPER" .... Iftiaz Haroon

"DR. BOMBAY" / JULIAN .... Greg Carere

CHUCK PETAL .... Starr Busby

JOHN (FROM THE NEW YORKER) / "BAMBI" .... Demetri Bonaros

"MR. BUNGLE" / MAN / "LEGBA (MALE)" .... Rob Erickson

IF YOU CAN GET TO BUFFALO was next produced by Son of Semele (Matthew McCray, Artistic Director) at Son of Semele Theater in Los Angeles, California on March 14, 2015. The performance was directed by Edgar Landa, with set design by Meg Cunningham, lights by Barbara Kallir, sound design by Becca Kessin, costume design by Hunter Wells, and projection design by Matthew McCray. The production stage manager was Lyndsay Lucas. The cast was as follows:

"STARSINGER" .... Cindy Nguyen

"LEGBA" .... Caitlin Teeley

"GRENDLEFISH" / "PURPLE GUEST" .... Betsy Moore

WIFE / "BILL GATES" .... Sarah Rosenberg

"JUNIPER" .... Chase Cargill

"DR. BOMBAY" / JULIAN .... Bart Petty

CHUCK PETAL .... Melina Bielefelt

JOHN (FROM THE NEW YORKER) / "BAMBI" .... Tim Venable

"MR. BUNGLE" / MAN / "LEGBA (MALE)" .... Alex Wells

CHARACTERS

The following should be played by eight actors.

"STARSINGER"

"DR. BOMBAY"

CHUCK PETAL

JULIAN

JOHN (FROM THE NEW YORKER)

"BAMBI"

"MR. BUNGLE"

WIFE

"BILL GATES"

"MAN"

"LEGBA" (MALE)

"LEGBA"

"JUNIPER"

"PURPLE GUEST" / "GRENDLEFISH"

One actor plays **"STARSINGER"**, another **"LEGBA"**, another **"JUNIPER"**.
The actor playing **"DR. BOMBAY"** also plays **JULIAN**.
The actor playing **JOHN (FROM THE NEW YORKER)** also plays **"BAMBI"**.
The actor playing **WIFE** also plays **"BILL GATES"** and **"PURPLE GUEST" / "GRENDLEFISH"**.
One actor plays **CHUCK PETAL**.
"MR. BUNGLE" plays **"MAN"** and **"LEGBA" (MALE)**.

NOTE ON SET AND COSTUME

The set needs to be very simple.

Everyone dresses kinda nerdy. And nineties. After all, this is 1993. It's nice if Starsinger's dress absolutely POPS when she changes into it.

NOTE ON SOUND

Sound should be detailed. The sound in this piece should help fill the emotional landscape.

> Text in boxes as headings, or to the right on the page, is projected. It describes either action or the different rooms that make up our virtual mansion.
>
> Text always scrolls from the bottom up.
> (If necessary because of spacing on a page, sometimes there is a "*" indicating start of scrolling text on the exact line usually indicating place.)

MORE NOTES

LambdaMOO was the first MOO (online chat room) of its kind, formed in 1990.

This play is inspired by actual events but is not an adaptation of real life. Creative liberties have been taken for dramatic purposes.

A "/" in dialogue indicates an overlap.

Mr. Bungle should be folding laundry, discretely watching the Chuck Petal episodes. When he exits for good, he carries his folded laundry with him.

Diverse casting is required.

For
Eric Nightengale
and
Katelin McMullin

1993: WELCOME TO LAMBDAMOO

(DR. BOMBAY, STARSINGER, LEGBA, GRENDLEFISH, *and* JUNIPER *enter.*)

(The disclaimer scrolls, music plays.*)

> *(Scrolling.)*
> You are a guest here on LamdaMOO.
> We are not responsible for your Good Time.
> You have no proof that anything we say is the absolute truth.
> You are not bound, tied up, unable to move,
> Your being here implies you are complacent.
> Everything you are about to hear,
> Everything you are participating in
> Is by your own doing.
> In the event of a complaint,
> Everything can be used against you,
> Is made public,
> Nothing is hidden.
> You make your own choices.
> We are not accountable.
> Please enjoy the show.

(JULIAN *walks into the spotlight. He's charming, but casual. He carries a small handheld recorder, the kind journalists use when taking notes for a story, which is what he's doing.*)

JULIAN. I always like to have, or to see, or to just overhear, the following in bars:
One person is like, "You HAD to be there."
And the other person goes, "No, I *totally know* what you're saying."
Then the first guy is usually like, "I hate to say this...but there's no way –"

---

*A license to produce *If You Can Get to Buffalo* does not include a performance license for any third-party or copyrighted music. Licensees should create an original composition or use music in the public domain. For further information, please see Music Use Note on page 3.

And *here* he gets cut off by his friend who just *insists* and insists that he can relate.
Look, man, I can relate.
Insisting and insisting that he *knows* what had happened.
I totally know, I totally know, I totally know.
I look at you, I can see it in your eyes man. It's like YIKES! WOW! I TOTALLY know.
And he wasn't even there.
But the other guy?
The one that was there?
It's very clear that he's the only one that *knows*.

They'll say that this, right here, this is pretty much a "you had to be there" situation.
    (A shift.)

YOU ENTER THROUGH THE COAT CLOSET

(**STARSINGER** *enters.*)

JULIAN. I found Starsinger in **The Coat Closet**.* She couldn't get out. If you don't know what you're doing, it's possible to never make it out of The Coat Closet... Which makes it an odd choice for the point of entry... But I wasn't making any rules on LambdaMOO – though I did add the bit –

(*Gestures casually to the scrolling text.*)

– about the Mohair Coats and Dirty Galoshes... And I added the part about looking for the latch...that they find it under the slick black raincoat...that they push the door, and that they are in awe, because they have entered:

The Living Room.

(**Fast scrolling.*)

THE COAT CLOSET: The closet is a dark, cramped space. It appears to be very crowded in here. It feels like coats, boots, and other people (apparently sleeping). There are Mohair Coats, Dirty Galoshes, proof that others have been there before you.

One useful thing that you've discovered in your bumbling about is a metal doorknob set at waist-level into what might be a door. Next to it is a spring lever labeled "QUIET!"

Not many find it because they don't know where to look, the determined know it's the only passage, they find the latch under the slick black raincoat, they push the door and they are in awe, because they've entered The Living Room.

7PM: THE PARTY IN THE LIVING ROOM

DR. BOMBAY. Welcome to **The Living Room**.* One can find literally anything they want in The Living Room. You see the Welcome Poster, a fireplace, the living room couch, Cockatoo, a pinball machine, a large mirror, and The Birthday Machine.

And tonight, like lots of nights, it was like a party –

LEGBA. *(Typing.) Party Music Starts.* Something classy and sophisticated, but also wild and unpredictable – like the slutty girl in high school that's from a really good family.*

JUNIPER. *(Typing.) The party has the sense of having both always been going on and of being the first of its kind. It's the party you've always wanted to go to but makes you a little nervous because everything's just exactly how you knew it would be.*

*(*Scrolling.)*
THE LIVING ROOM: It is very bright, open, and airy here, with large plate-glass windows looking southward over the pool to the gardens beyond. On the north wall, there is a rough stonework fireplace. There is a coffee table with a Monopoly board on it. The east and west walls are almost completely covered with large, well-stocked bookcases. There are two sets of couches, one clustered around the fireplace and one with a view out the windows. You see the Welcome Poster, a fireplace, the living room couch, Cockatoo, pinball machine, a large mirror, and The Birthday Machine.

GRENDLEFISH. *(Typing.) Grendlefish can't believe all the compliments she's gotten on her crop top, and, as the Twilight-Zone-pinball-machine-top-scorer-in-the-whole-world, she knows for a fact that the sweet smell of success is nothing compared to a night with friends in The Living Room.*

STARSINGER. *(Typing.) Starsinger is the girl that dressed up a little TOO much for the party. She looks fabulous, but a bit uncomfortable, and lets out a 1930s cocktail party laugh and throws her head back.*

(Shift.)

What's that?

DR. BOMBAY. Pickled okra.

STARSINGER. I didn't know this party had /
okra?

DR. BOMBAY. Pickled okra.

STARSINGER. I have mixed feelings about
pickled okra...

---

*A license to produce *If You Can Get to Buffalo* does not include a performance license for any third-party or copyrighted music. Licensees should create an original composition or use music in the public domain. For further information, please see Music Use Note on page 3.

DR. BOMBAY. Why.

STARSINGER. I just...want it to be a pickle.

DR. BOMBAY. Well, as long as it's not cheese.

STARSINGER. No way!

Apparently the Dutch are the only ones that are supposed to eat cheese. Because of –

(Beat.)

Evolution. Their bodies have adapted or whatever. / To cheese.

DR. BOMBAY. Ugh, I drank SO much hibiscus tea yesterday

> LEGBA teleports in.

STARSINGER. Kinda like why Europeans are so tiny.
Smaller stature.

GRENDLEFISH. I really love you guys!

DR. BOMBAY. It's just all a continuous loop / isn't it.

STARSINGER. Living in close quarters to livestock and stuff.

LEGBA. Too much hibiscus can be danger / ous.

STARSINGER. Like / years ago.

LEGBA. Apparently.

DR. BOMBAY. *(To* **STARSINGER.***)* Legba, a Haitian witch. Her long black dreadlocks change color depending on her mood. She's usually found in The Kitchen, it's very comfortable, has a little breakfast nook with a table and four chairs, beautiful natural-wood cabinets, and a stove set into a very large island counter. She's come because word has been spreading that there's a performance... She's decided to grace us tonight, in The Living Room.

> *(**STARSINGER** smiles and waves to **LEGBA**.)*

STARSINGER. Hi!
I love / your name.

> STARSINGER smiles and waves!

LEGBA. *(In an "eh, the-new-girl-how-annoying" sort of way.)* Legba.

DR. BOMBAY. Starsinger's performing. Tonight, ten o'clock. / You're early.

LEGBA. I heard.

JUNIPER. Starsinger's performing!

> JUNIPER teleports in.

DR. BOMBAY. *(To* **STARSINGER**.*)* Juniper! A Squirrel.
I think he / drinks a lot.

LEGBA. What is it exactly?

JUNIPER. Tonight, / ten o'clock.

DR. BOMBAY. A performance –

STARSINGER. A song.
I suppose?

DR. BOMBAY. *(To all.)* The performance will start soon –

STARSINGER. Maybe this is too soon? /
Tomorrow, maybe tomorrow?

DR. BOMBAY. Starsinger's Famous.

JUNIPER. I heard her once, in / in Paris, I think.

STARSINGER. I sang in Rome once.

LEGBA. I was famous once.

> **LEGBA** floats up to the ceiling.

GRENDLEFISH. Hey, good for you!

STARSINGER. Then you know!

LEGBA. I was famous for going from here... to there.

JUNIPER. Are you sure that's right?

> **(STARSINGER** *can't control herself yet.)*

> **STARSINGER** smiles and waves!

LEGBA. From here to / there.

JUNIPER. Oh, I've been *there*.

> **STARSINGER** smiles and waves!

LEGBA. Exactly.

I was like the snail. That snail in *Pinocchio*.

> **STARSINGER** smiles and waves!

STARSINGER. There's a snail in *Pinocchio*?

> *(Beat.)*

> **STARSINGER** smiles and waves!
> **STARSINGER** smiles and waves!

LEGBA. That *famous* snail.

> **STARSINGER** smiles and waves!
> **STARSINGER** smiles and waves!

> *(Beat.)*

> **STARSINGER** smiles and waves!
> **STARSINGER** smiles and waves!

There's that snail
and the snail invites Pinocchio to his house.

> **STARSINGER** smiles and waves!
> **STARSINGER** smiles and waves!

Pinocchio's like, awesome I get to go to the snail's / house –

STARSINGER. *(To self, confused.)* I can't stop "smiling and waving!"

LEGBA. – Then the snail takes nine hours to reach the front door. Be careful what you wish for is all I'm saying, you know?

DR. BOMBAY. Sounds like you had to have been there. / Who needs a drink?

LEGBA. I need a / drink.

JUNIPER. I *have* a drink –

STARSINGER. How do we drink?

LEGBA. Through that hole in your ear.

JUNIPER. – But I'll have another.

GRENDLEFISH. Just water for me.

STARSINGER. And I'll have Champagne.

> **(DR. BOMBAY** *walks over to the bar.)*

> **(MR. BUNGLE** *appears.)*

DR. BOMBAY. What Living Room would be complete without a **Puppet Bar*** complete with a bartender with a penchant for language! Everyone was quite fond of this silly creature. Everyone likes a quiet, brooding poet.

> *THE PUPPET BAR: In the back, upper pocket of The Living Room is the Puppet Bar. Banks of strange-looking monitoring equipment, flashing lights, screens, buttons, dials, and other bits of foreign objects are flanked with dusty red curtains and bottles of tequila. The bartender, Mr. Bungle, wears a clown white face and silly hat.
>
> Mr. Bungle's Puppet Show is always going on. People just choose to tune in occasionally.

Bungle, Legba would like turquoise Champagne, extra olives, no umbrella, and a dry hot rye for Starsinger – we must preserve her voice. I'm sure you know what Juniper is having, one water, and I'll have...Cristal.

(They all turn to watch – they are used to his shows.)

MR. BUNGLE. Mr. Bungle here. Excuse me if I don't make eye contact, I can't look directly at things. I have a rapidly accelerating hereditary degenerative disease called Extreme Empathy. I feel sorry for staplers. For burning candles. For dogs that can't bark. I can't handle it. I shut my eyes as tight as possible and hum. All the while feeling sorry for snakes, they can see through their eyelids.

I liked these people, here in The Living Room. It was that simple. They are squirrels, witches, dolphins. I had everything I needed right here. In my house. I had a phone. I had things brought to me. I ordered in. I liked sushi. That's how it worked.

But do not be confused. I pride myself on my intelligence. I try not to get too bored. I know what boredom leads to...*possibility*. I now know that whales had legs and that penguins can jump six feet in the air, and here, I get to be both of them.

On LambdaMOO I never age, not a day. I watch and listen. I woke up. The Birthday Machine says I'm 1,008...94...34...16. In my clown white face, with my Bisquick breath – I was about to have some fun and I couldn't wait to see what they would do.

(Scrolling.)

Mr. Bungle here. Excuse me if I don't make eye contact, I can't look directly at things. I have a rapidly accelerating hereditary degenerative disease called Extreme Empathy. I feel sorry for staplers. For burning candles. For dogs that can't bark. I can't handle it. I shut my eyes as tight as possible and hum. All the while feeling sorry for snakes, they can see through their eyelids.

I liked these people, here in The Living Room. It was that simple. They are squirrels, witches, dolphins. I had everything I needed right here. In my house. I had a phone. I had things brought to me. I ordered in. I liked sushi. That's how it worked.

But do not be confused. I pride myself on my intelligence. I try not to get too bored. I know what boredom leads to...*possibility*. I now know that whales had legs and that penguins can jump six feet in the air, and here, I get to be both of them.

On LambdaMOO I never age, not a day. I watch and listen. I woke up. The Birthday Machine says I'm 1,008...94...34...16. In my clown white face, with my Bisquick breath – I was about to have some fun and I couldn't wait to see what they would do.

THE CHUCK PETAL SHOW

(November 1994. The Chuck Petal Show. Sound Effects: Chuck Petal show intro music.*)

(CHUCK, JOHN (FROM THE NEW YORKER), *and* **JULIAN.)**

(Ever so faintly **MR. BUNGLE** *is present onstage [during all three of these scenes, folding his laundry].)*

CHUCK PETAL. Good evening. Quite a show we have, almost futuristic. I'm Chuck Petal, and tonight I'm sitting here with John from *The New Yorker* and a young writer named Julian.

JULIAN. Great to be here.

*(***JOHN** *just nods.)*

CHUCK PETAL. *(To* **JOHN.***)* You recently had an article in *The New Yorker* that garnered a lot of attention about this "electronic mail" and Inter-net and what it all is. Actually, tell us what it is, this Inter-net, before we get down to your electronic mail thing.

JOHN. Sure, the internet, like many things, has a specific meaning. This meaning is rapidly changing as more people get involved. The internet PROPER is a computer network, established by the government in the late seventies.

CHUCK PETAL. Ahhhh, the late seventies.

JOHN. Now, today, in 1994, there are 33,000 separate online networks that have all been connected to this one BIG network –

CHUCK PETAL. Inter-net.

JOHN. – Called the internet.

CHUCK PETAL. And, electronic mail?

JOHN. *E-mail.*

CHUCK PETAL. E-mail. So – you send a message and somebody responds. You send a message and somebody responds. You send a message and somebody responds, you send –

JULIAN. A message and someone responds. Yes. Personally, one element I have been specifically aware of and interested in is a MUD.

CHUCK PETAL. You are interested in mud.

JULIAN. Multi-User Dimensions. One type of a MUD is a MOO – Multi-User Dimension Object-Oriented. MOO.

CHUCK PETAL. A MOO.

JULIAN. These are social networks, they provide a place where people from anywhere can log on – entirely through text – and enter a landscape where they can interact. A mountain, a mansion, a Living Room. People adopt certain roles, they have intense erotic relationships –

---

*A license to produce *If You Can Get to Buffalo* does not include a performance license for any third-party or copyrighted music. Licensees should create an original composition or use music in the public domain. For further information, please see Music Use Note on page 3.

CHUCK PETAL. How does one have an "intense erotic relationship."

> (**JULIAN** *laughs awkwardly.*)

JULIAN. Well, ha, Chuck – how do YOU have an intense erotic relationship.

> (*Beat.*)

CHUCK PETAL. (*To* **JOHN.**) Didn't you once assume the role of...a woman.

JOHN. Yes. I did. Her name was Bambi.

CHUCK PETAL. *Your* name was Bambi.

JOHN. Yes. My name –

CHUCK PETAL. Her name –

JOHN. – Her name –

CHUCK PETAL. You –

JOHN. My name –

CHUCK PETAL. *Her* name –

JOHN. – *Her* name –

CHUCK PETAL. You –

JOHN. *WE*, were Bambi.

> (*Beat.*)

CHUCK PETAL. What did you discover?

JOHN. Men are very aggressive.

CHUCK PETAL. Was your wife thrilled about this.

JOHN. I did this in the company of my wife.

CHUCK PETAL. Was she pleased.

JOHN. Yeah, she was kind of pleased.

CHUCK PETAL. So she liked it immensely.

JOHN. I don't think she considered it to be infidelity of any kind.

CHUCK PETAL. (*Chuckles.*) Bambi.

JOHN. I only did it because I was too lazy to come on to the girls, I'd rather have the guys come on to me.

CHUCK PETAL. And did they? Did the "guys" come on to you?

> (*Shift.*)

("BAMBI" [JOHN (FROM THE NEW YORKER)] *is sitting at a "bar."* WIFE *is by his side.)*

(When WIFE *speaks, it is very suggestive, seductive, at half volume. She is prompting* "BAMBI". *If there is a "//" in* "MAN"'s *dialogue this is when* WIFE *overlaps.* "MAN" *overlaps with "/".)*

("MAN" [MR. BUNGLE] *enters and sits very close to "BAMBI.")*

(Super cheesy bar music.)*

MAN. Heyyyyyyyyyyyy.

WIFE. *(To* BAMBI.) *Hello there.*

BAMBI. *(Typing.)* Hello there.

MAN. Well hi, who are you?

WIFE. *Bambi.*

BAMBI. ...Bambi.

MAN. Of course you are.
   First time here.

WIFE. *It's my first time here.*

BAMBI. It's my first time here.

MAN. Do // you like it?

WIFE. *Do you like / it?*

BAMBI. Do you like it?

MAN. Yeah.

WIFE. *Yeah.*

BAMBI. Yeah.

MAN. A // Lot.

WIFE. *Good.*

BAMBI. Good.

MAN. Gooo // ooooooooood.

WIFE. *I'm sure I like / it.*

BAMBI. I'm sure I / like it.

MAN. Tell me about yourself.

WIFE. *There's so much to tell.*

---

*A license to produce *If You Can Get to Buffalo* does not include a performance license for any third-party or copyrighted music. Licensees should create an original composition or use music in the public domain. For further information, please see Music Use Note on page 3.

BAMBI. There's so much to tell –

    (Looking at **WIFE** *with shrug.* **WIFE** *is encouraging.)*

WIFE. I'm a little –

BAMBI. I'm...a little...

    *(***WIFE** *mimes "hot in here.")*

WIFE. HOT.

MAN. ...Hot.

    *(***WIFE** *mimes "hot in here" harder.)*

WIFE. *Is it hot in here?*

BAMBI. Is it hot in here?

    (Shrugs at **WIFE.***)*

MAN. You're wearing a dress.
  I like your / dress.

BAMBI. Dress!

    *(***WIFE** *smiles and nods.)*

MAN. Maybe you should take it off.
  If you're hot I mean.

BAMBI. My.

MAN. Are there buttons on it?

WIFE. *So many.*

MAN. Millions of little buttons running down the front...

WIFE. *Buttons.*

BAMBI. So many...
  Buttons.

MAN. There are too many buttons.
  The dress was created around your fit...body.

    *(***WIFE** *laughs, this is funny shit.)*

  Too... So... All those...

BAMBI. I could –

MAN. ...Many buttons.

WIFE. *I could just pull it over my head.*

    *(***WIFE** *mimes taking the dress off over her head.)*

BAMBI. I could just pull it over my head / that might be easier?

MAN. Oh yeah. / Do it.

WIFE. *There, that's much better.*

BAMBI. ...There, that's much better.

WIFE. *Are you hot?*

BAMBI. Are you...hot?

MAN. Tell me about your tits.

BAMBI. Excuse me??

    *(***WIFE** *slugs* **BAMBI** *on arm. He tries not to laugh.)*

MAN. Are they loose, are your nipples hard or are they all // bunched up overflowing your black bra...

WIFE. *Loose –*

BAMBI. Loose –

    (Looks helplessly at **WIFE.***)*

WIFE. *Hard.*

BAMBI. HARD?!

MAN. Me too.

WIFE. *MYYYYYYYYYY.*

BAMBI. My.

MAN. Come sit on my lap.

BAMBI. What?

MAN. I need you to SIT on my lap.

    *(***WIFE*** shakes head "yes."* **WIFE** *leads* **BAMBI** *and literally sits* **BAMBI** *on* **MAN***'s lap, but no eye contact is made.)*

BAMBI. Yes, I'm...

MAN. I know / I can feel you.

WIFE. *Sitting on your lap.*

BAMBI. Sitting on your lap.

MAN. Can you feel that.

WIFE. *I do.*

MAN. Do you feel that.

BAMBI. I do.

MAN. You dirty fucking bitch –

WIFE. *I'm a dirty fucking bitch.*

BAMBI. I'm...a...dirty fucking bitch –

MAN. Yeah –

WIFE. *Yeah.*

BAMBI. Yeah –

MAN. Yeah –

WIFE. *Yeah.*

BAMBI. Yeah.

MAN. Fuck.
    FUCK!
    / Fuckfuckfuckfuck –

    *(***WIFE*** and ***BAMBI*** are silently dying laughing.* **MAN** *is so, so deadly serious.)*

BAMBI. Oh –

WIFE. *OH!*

MAN. JESUS –

WIFE. *Myy / yyyyyyyyyy.*

BAMBI. Mymy / mymy –

MAN. So –

BAMBI. My that feels –

WIFE. *So / good.*

MAN. – So good.

WIFE. *Oh, yes –*

BAMBI. Oh, yes.

It.

Does.

WIFE. *Oh, yes –*

BAMBI. Oh, yes.

It

does...

(**MAN** *is making noises...* **WIFE** *starts kissing* **BAMBI**, *clearly turned on.*)

MAN. There's a party...in Buffalo.

I'd like to meet you there.

THE CHUCK PETAL SHOW

JOHN. *(To* **CHUCK PETAL**.*)* I have to tell you, having had the experience being a woman for a half hour...I *actually* think I learned a little.

CHUCK PETAL. Did you engage in sex?

JOHN. I...let a guy kind of do it to me.

CHUCK PETAL. Did your wife enjoy that.

JOHN. Sorry?

CHUCK PETAL. Well.

JOHN. Yeah...

(**JULIAN** *quietly laughs.*)

You know, it was really...forceful.

CHUCK PETAL. *Manly.*

(Beat.)

JOHN. *Forceful.* But interesting.

CHUCK PETAL. I'm sure your wife found it interesting. Did he want to meet you in real life?

(**JOHN** *awkward laughs.*)

JOHN. Well, he did send me an invitation to a party in Buffalo...

(Beat.)

CHUCK PETAL. *(To* **JULIAN**.*)* Julian. Tell me, you were involved with a case of "rape."

JULIAN. I wasn't "involved" exactly.

CHUCK PETAL. What happened.

JULIAN. Well, it's a variation on this common theme that's in all of these types of communities.

CHUCK PETAL. Rape communities.

JULIAN. People feel they can hide behind anonymity or pseudonymity and get away with things.

CHUCK PETAL. Rape.

JULIAN. This guy was particularly creative. See, you can SAY things on LambdaMOO or you can DO actions. So, for instance, I'm Dr. Bombay. So, I type "Dr. Bombay jumps off the ceiling" and what they read – some dude in Australia sitting at his computer for example – what he sees on the screen is, "Dr. Bombay jumps off the ceiling."

>*(Beat.)*

CHUCK PETAL. ...What?

JULIAN. What this guy – Mr. Bungle – was able to do, was send messages to people in the room that made it appear as if others were performing sexual acts on him.

CHUCK PETAL. *(To* **JOHN.***)* Bet your wife would like that!

>*(To* **JULIAN.***)* Which acts were performed?

JULIAN. What?

CHUCK PETAL. Which sexual acts?

JULIAN. Well, it's not, it's, let's see – they were very violent. And non-traditional.

CHUCK PETAL. A three-way?

JULIAN. There were knives involved.

CHUCK PETAL. Fascinating. So. This guy, your Mr. Bungle, he has become like the conductor of his own little sex opera.

JULIAN. *(Oh no, he thinks he's being funny...)* Well, sure – if the opera's called RAPE if you know what I mean.

>*(Beat.)*

CHUCK PETAL. So, there was a panic. What do people do when this occurs?

JULIAN. It's unprecedented, they weren't sure.

CHUCK PETAL. Can't you simply leave the room.

JULIAN. There is no "room" –

CHUCK PETAL. Turn off your computer.

JULIAN. It's not that simple.

CHUCK PETAL. Close your eyes.

JULIAN. This was a violation. See – these people had been living in their own new world. They had finally found IT – the tree house for adults, the make-believe that was real, the ultimate choose your own adventure... It's naive, but at the time, it didn't seem possible that anyone involved would be anything other than a congenial good-natured member of an exclusive club –

CHUCK PETAL. In the tree house.

JULIAN. – And now everyone is having to deal with a real-world situation and it was confusing for them. For us.

CHUCK PETAL. And these were poor and disabled people from around the world.

JULIAN. ...No!

CHUCK PETAL. People whose daily struggle we could not begin to understand.

JULIAN. Chuck.

CHUCK PETAL. People who tried to work hard and care for their families, secretly scared that there was a plot to eliminate the underclasses, globally.

JULIAN. *(Almost laughing.)* Chuck –

CHUCK PETAL. *(To camera.)* I've done many segments on this subject folks. Predators. Prey. Tree houses. People need to monitor their children, keep an eye on what little Johnny is doing, 'cause someone might be trying to get into little Johnny's pants.

    (Beat.)

We'll be right back with Chuck Petal.

8PM: THE PARTY IN THE LIVING ROOM

(JUNIPER and LEGBA are having the most interesting conversation they can think of to have.)

(The music is picking up... This party's getting "wild." **PURPLE GUEST** *will soon enter.)*

> THE LIVING ROOM: It is very bright, open, and airy here, with large plate-glass windows looking southward over the pool to the gardens beyond. On the north wall, there is a rough stonework fireplace. There is a coffee table with a Monopoly board on it. The east and west walls are almost completely covered with large, well-stocked bookcases. There are two sets of couches, one clustered around the fireplace and one with a view out the windows. You see the Welcome Poster, a fireplace, the living room couch, Cockatoo, pinball machine, a large mirror, and The Birthday Machine.

JUNIPER. Here's something I'm sure you don't know...
I drink a lot of water.
Tons of it.
Can't get enough.
When I'm sitting there with my glass, when I look over and see that my water pitcher seems empty?
I immediately fill it.
And then I'll pour myself a glass and then *I* drink that glass.
And then I'll refill it.
I just can't get enough of the stuff.
I like to hydrate / – feel like a million bucks when I'm hydrated.

LEGBA. Hydrate? Huh.
Do you nap? / Are you a napper?

JUNIPER. Oh, ha! I love pillows! Most think that the pillow has no feelings whatsoever about the frequency of an afternoon napper, but I have it on good authority / that they enjoy it.

LEGBA. Pillows are bad / for you.

JUNIPER. *(Really explaining this.)* Pillows *enjoy* the nap.

LEGBA. Neck Shit.

JUNIPER. "Pillows Enjoy / The Nap!"

LEGBA. Pillows mess up Neck Shit.

> **PURPLE GUEST** teleports in.

PURPLE GUEST. Hi Friends.

LEGBA. Why do you keep doing that.

PURPLE GUEST. I'm hungry?

LEGBA. You keep coming as PURPLE GUEST.

JUNIPER. She's / new –

LEGBA. She's not new.

JUNIPER. You're not looking for a copywriter are you? / I write A LOT of marketing copy. I'm pretty good at it.

PURPLE GUEST. I like "Purple Guest" /
I had purple hair in high school

JUNIPER. My father's father was actually in the marketing copy market and I hear that sometimes it skips a generation so I'm going into marketing with a / concentration on the copy though.

LEGBA. I didn't go to high school.
Straight to college.

JUNIPER. On marketing copy.
Do you like pillows?

PURPLE GUEST. Purple pillows.

JUNIPER. Let me try some copy out.
Or I'll say something and you let me know if you / think it's *copy* or not.

LEGBA. Just *go* / already.

PURPLE GUEST. Games aren't really my deal /
But –

JUNIPER. *(Clears throat. Ahem.)* "Pristine beaches are the home to the blue, blue waves
that lap up to their shore. Just a short flight away one
is all of a sudden in a paradise of dreams. Hush,
listen to the soft hum of the locals playing their indigenous
instruments. Let it lull you to sleep in a bed of purple pillows.
Let us go to iconic Florida.
This summer, cum in Florida's mouth."

    (PURPLE GUEST *starts laughing.)*

PURPLE GUEST. Oh my god. *Copy.*

    (Shift.)

LEGBA teleports out.

IN THE LIVING ROOM, ON THE COUCH, NEAR THE FIREPLACE

(The party music is still on, but now muffled in the background.)

STARSINGER. *(Typing.) Starsinger has been inspecting the bookcase in The Living Room, casually leafing through first editions.*
Dr. Bombay had been watching her with interest.
They now sit very close together.

JULIAN. *(Out.)* One of my favorite things about LamdaMOO is that if you want a moment of privacy, like if you just want to talk to one person instead of the entire world hearing you, you can.
And I did.
With Starsinger.

STARSINGER. – And I've always dreamed of like –

JULIAN. She's telling me about *feelings* or something.

STARSINGER. Ah, a limo?

JULIAN. I've just been smiling and nodding and trying to think of something clever to say.

STARSINGER. But like
a Limo /
SUV thing, you know?

DR. BOMBAY. I just bought you one / I hope you like pink.

STARSINGER. No!!
So tonight
I'll be sitting there
in my chair
in my room
and a sleek pink limousine might glide through the window to pick me up?

DR. BOMBAY. That's exactly what I'm saying.
SkyMall.

STARSINGER. SkyMall?

DR. BOMBAY. I purchased the pink limo SUV from / SkyMall...

STARSINGER. ...The in-flight magazine thing?

DR. BOMBAY. *(?)*
They have *really* cool stuff...

     (Beat.)

So.
Are you ready –

STARSINGER. I'm / nervous.

DR. BOMBAY. Don't be nervous.

STARSINGER. Have you / ever –

DR. BOMBAY jumps off the ceiling.

DR. BOMBAY. Yes.

STARSINGER. Have you ever felt like you knew someone completely?

DR. BOMBAY. Someone I know?

STARSINGER. Know someone completely.

DR. BOMBAY. Only for a while, when I first meet them.

STARSINGER. You know them completely.

DR. BOMBAY. After the first intimate conversation.
That's the only time.

STARSINGER. After you've told a secret?

DR. BOMBAY. No –

STARSINGER. Or maybe just before?

DR. BOMBAY. After the first laugh.
But before the first secret.

STARSINGER. I see.

DR. BOMBAY. After the first laugh.
Before the first put-down.
In that space.

STARSINGER. Is there a story involved?

DR. BOMBAY. There's a song involved.
Do you know my favorite song?

STARSINGER. No.

DR. BOMBAY. Oh, it's a great song.

STARSINGER. Tell me.

DR. BOMBAY. I may not look like it, but I'm a musical theatre nut.
I like the old ones, with heart.

STARSINGER. Don't the new ones have heart?

DR. BOMBAY. It's not the same.
I'm not afraid of a little nostalgia, you know?

STARSINGER. I...think so?

DR. BOMBAY. I'm not afraid of say, Judy Garland.

STARSINGER. I'm not afraid of Judy Garland.

DR. BOMBAY. Some people are though.

STARSINGER. Oh...

DR. BOMBAY. My absolute favorite song is "Look for the Silver Lining." Just...*perception*, right?
One person sees something like this.
Then another sees something like that.
Then the other maybe squints a bit and is like, oh...wow...sure, I think I see it different.
Thanks.

STARSINGER. "Look for the Silver Lining."
I wonder if I should learn / to sing it.

DR. BOMBAY. You should learn to sing it.
It could change the way you think about everything.
Do you read?

STARSINGER. Of course.

>   (**STARSINGER** *slowly hums a bit of the song, trying to figure it out, but in a not too distracting sort of way.*)

DR. BOMBAY. Are you ever reading a book, and then you're realizing after you've finished, you're like – HUH. That book was all about *me*.

> **STARSINGER** stares off to the middle distance.

I was the subject and I didn't even know it.
And then you're telling your friend about the book,
about how it's YOU in the book,
about how which you it is, and not until you tell him –
is it real.

STARSINGER. No.

DR. BOMBAY. So you never feel like we are already in the future?

STARSINGER. I think I'll learn that song.

DR. BOMBAY. Will you credit me?

STARSINGER. Credit / you?

DR. BOMBAY. Tonight, at your show, when you walk out on stage,

> **STARSINGER** floats to the ceiling.

when the spotlight is on you
and you're just about to sing the first words
will you say,
"I wouldn't be here tonight if Dr. Bombay hadn't introduced me to this first number, here's to him."

>   (*Beat.*)

Then you'll start singing?

>   (*Beat.*)

STARSINGER. Um.
I need to prepare.

>   (**STARSINGER** *turns out of scene and applies some lipstick, slowly.*)

>   (*Shift.*)

JULIAN. (*Out.*) They say the events of the evening went down "at or about 10 p.m. Pacific Standard Time."
That seems right to me.
As promised, soon Starsinger will be picked up by a brand-new pink SUV limo.
Her show will start at 9:58 and last roughly four minutes.
She will wear a red dress.
The kind of dress she's always seen herself in.
She can imagine years and years later
this dress will be auctioned off to the highest bidder,
someone who wants a piece of history.
For a while, everyone will have the greatest time they have ever had.

>   (*Shift.*)

DR. BOMBAY. I'm thirsty, let's see how our Mr. Bungle is doing… It's only eight o'clock.

(**DR. BOMBAY** *walks over to the bar. Our bartender puppet* **MR. BUNGLE** *appears.*)

Fill me up my friend. How Now Brown Cow?

(*They all turn to watch as he makes their drinks and speaks.*)

THE PUPPET BAR: In the back, upper pocket of The Living Room is the Puppet Bar. Banks of strange-looking monitoring equipment, flashing lights, screens, buttons, dials, and other bits of foreign objects are flanked with dusty red curtains and bottles of tequila. The bartender, Mr. Bungle, wears a clown white face and silly hat.

Mr. Bungle's Puppet Show is always going on. People just choose to tune in occasionally.

MR. BUNGLE. Mr. Bungle here. An arrogant French philosopher once equated boredom to the beauty of a young gentleman who "yawns and walks around with a butterfly net to catch goldfish." His young man "carries in his pocket a pedometer, a pair of nail scissors, a pack of cards, and all sorts of games based on optical illusions."

My pockets contain pictures from magazines of blond women on brown couches, of a television the size of my front door and a coupon for a free pacemaker, when you buy two more.

Our Frenchman asks questions about good and evil, happy and sad. I see him wrapped with a blanket sitting on a wooden chair. He lives in a trailer but calls it a cabin; he doesn't see the wheels.

I feel nothing towards him as I turn and squint to see through the window noticing the red-headed stranger pull on her backpack, lock her front door and smile to herself as she turns up the street. Maybe I'll be her today. Have white flesh and white teeth and worry about what I'll be when I grow up.

(*Scrolling.*)

Mr. Bungle here. An arrogant French philosopher once equated boredom to the beauty of a young gentleman who "yawns and walks around with a butterfly net to catch goldfish." His young man "carries in his pocket a pedometer, a pair of nail scissors, a pack of cards, and all sorts of games based on optical illusions."

My pockets contain pictures from magazines of blond women on brown couches, of a television the size of my front door and a coupon for a free pacemaker, when you buy two more.

Our Frenchman asks questions about good and evil, happy and sad. I see him wrapped with a blanket sitting on a wooden chair. He lives in a trailer but calls it a cabin; he doesn't see the wheels.

I feel nothing towards him as I turn and squint to see through the window noticing the red-headed stranger pull on her backpack, lock her front door and smile to herself as she turns up the street. Maybe I'll be her today. Have white flesh and white teeth and worry about what I'll be when I grow up.

THE (SAME) CHUCK PETAL SHOW

(**CHUCK** and **JOHN** are sharing a hearty laugh.)

CHUCK PETAL. (Laughing.) Absolutely right you are! You *New Yorker* guys. God. Alright, when we come back, we'll STILL be talking about Inter-net. Everybody else is, and so will we. Back in a moment when we'll see what's happening on "the net."

(There's an indication they are off air.)

"The Net." Hope you guys are having fun on the show...

JULIAN. This is the future Chuck –

CHUCK PETAL. That's what they said about Tang.

JULIAN. Tang?

CHUCK PETAL. They said, John Glenn you take Tang to the moon and everyone will drink Tang.

JOHN. Who said that?

CHUCK PETAL. I don't drink Tang. Do you?

JOHN. Well, no.

CHUCK PETAL. You?

JULIAN. No...but this is different –

JOHN. Chuck, you'll look back on this and laugh.

(**JOHN** awkward laughs.)

CHUCK PETAL. What?

JOHN. Look back, on this, and laugh.

CHUCK PETAL. I'll look back on this and laugh?

JOHN. You'll look back on this and laugh –

CHUCK PETAL. Tang!

JULIAN. We can back up if it seems complicated, go over some of the basics again –

(An indicator that **CHUCK** is back on air.)

CHUCK PETAL. Imagine a place where people are judged not by age or gender or by the color of their skin, but by their words alone. It might sound like a utopia, on the international computer network known as "Inter-net" you can be whomever you choose. This virtual community can make for some very interesting scenarios.

People fall in love with those they've never seen. Some find the friend they thought was a woman is really a man. Some have Intense Erotic Relationships, while still others find themselves right at home, perhaps in the living room with their wife, listening to opera while getting virtually gang banged –

(Glancing at **JOHN**.)

– and liking it.

(Beat.)

So, this brings me back around to you Julian, or Dr. Bombay, or whatever. When you say "He raped them that night," really, what exactly do you mean?

JULIAN. Mr. Bungle had the ability –

CHUCK PETAL. Because it's not as if they were in the same room.

JULIAN. Well, no –

CHUCK PETAL. So –

JULIAN. He created a Voodoo doll –

CHUCK PETAL. A Voodoo doll.

(Awkward laugh.)

This is all a bit out of the realm of normal thinking, don't you think?

JULIAN. It's a code that –

CHUCK PETAL. This is a very *sensitive subject.*

(Beat.)

If I look at you and yell "I AM RAPING YOU," the question is – did I rape you?

JULIAN. It's more complicated –

Yes, *they* did.

CHUCK PETAL. Do you feel violated?

JULIAN. Some of them did. See, he had the ability to make them do things that / they couldn't control.

CHUCK PETAL. So, did they send him to prison?

JULIAN. No, of course not –

(Flashes smile.)

– they summoned the wizards –

CHUCK PETAL. The wizards.

JOHN. The computer programmers –

JULIAN. The wizards created the MOO, and for a long time left it to self-govern… They felt that socially, people should be able to create their own rules. So the wizards came in and said – "Hey, you guys need to find a way to deal with this yourself." What Mr. Bungle had done was, ah, violate three or four people in the room that night –

CHUCK PETAL. "Non-traditional sexual acts / involving knives."

JULIAN. But the wizards wanted them to get together to discuss how they *felt.* As a collective, as a society, they had to decide what the rules were, what was allowed. This was uncharted territory Chuck.

CHUCK PETAL. Like the Louisiana Purchase.

JULIAN. There was a lot of discussion about what sort of system they would have. No one had thought in these, well, terms. Big ticket items. Principles.

CHUCK PETAL. FDR.

JULIAN. Foundations.

CHUCK PETAL. Mortar and stone.

JULIAN. Civilizations.

CHUCK PETAL. The Incas.

JULIAN. Would it be a democracy? A parliament? What had started as this cool escape, this retreat into another world per se, was winding up with the same rules, the same constraints.

(Beat.)

JULIAN. I think, I think, I think people were *surprised* that when they *finally* settled on pretty much a direct democracy...democracy was disappointing.

    (Beat.)

So, they Toaded him.

CHUCK PETAL. They "Toaded" him.

JULIAN. MOO vernacular. To Toad someone is to, well, delete them.

    (Beat.)

They are gone.

JOHN. What Julian is saying is –

CHUCK PETAL. What Julian is saying is that if the Incas built a castle out of mortar and stone for FDR, we'd all be having a lot more sex.

    (Shaking his head.)

Let's break for a moment, and when we come back maybe I'll grab a camera guy, some Tang, and teleport up to Saturn to show everyone what the earth looks like first-hand from outer space.

STARSINGER. *(Typing.) Starsinger's never been to The Dining Room before. Actually, she's rather new on LambdaMOO...*

LEGBA. *(Typing.) Legba morphs into a fish that can exist both inside the fishbowl and outside the aquarium. Of course she likes the rocks on the floor, the way the sunlight reflects off the greens and reds and yellows, but on certain days, like Thursdays, she prefers the wind through her hair and would rather walk to school than swim...*

STARSINGER. Hello?

Hello?

LEGBA. Oh, Hi.

STARSINGER. Hey!

LEGBA. What's up?

STARSINGER. Nada...

Hanging out.

LEGBA. Me too!

So, where are you from?

STARSINGER. Seattle –

LEGBA. I'm from Mass.

STARSINGER. Cool. / Nice.

LEGBA. Do you like it here?

STARSINGER. Yeah, it's good, do you come to LambdaMOO / much, or, often?

LEGBA. Every now and again.

How old are you?

STARSINGER. Twenty-eight. You?

LEGBA. I'm twenty.

I'm Jill, by the way.

STARSINGER. Starsinger.

LEGBA. Nice to meet you Starsinger.

Is this your first time here?

STARSINGER. In The Dining Room? Yes.

THE DINING ROOM is dominated by a large pearwood table and six matching chairs. On the north wall is a large bookcase, flanked on each side by French doors leading northwest to the drawing room and northeast to the smoking room. The kitchen is visible through a similar pair of doors to the south, and a large, open archway leads east into the entrance hall. Piled on a bench in one corner is a Mastermind Board, Mastermind instructions, Deck of Playing Cards, Automatic Poker Pot, zoologist, Acquire, Set Game, Quarto, Wooden Chest of Games, Frand's backgammon board, Number puzzle, an Iron Puzzle, Frand's mind bender, Game of Hearts, Twister™, Ghost game, Frand's chessboard, Frand's reversi board, Snap's Connect Four board, Solitaire, gess board, go board, Rubik's Cube, Rog's solver for Frand's mind bender, Crazy Eight Ball, and an old coin.

LEGBA smiles and waves!

STARSINGER smiles and waves!

I was in The Coat Closet first. Then, remember, The Living Room /

I have no idea what I'm doing –

LEGBA. / Funny how you just wandered into The Living Room?

STARSINGER. But before, I was stuck in The / Coat Closet.

LEGBA. There's a lot of cool people here.

STARSINGER. Like / Dr. Bombay yeah –

LEGBA. Want to find somewhere with more personality?

STARSINGER. Sure, where?

I feel like I'm / bad at teleporting –

LEGBA. I can bring you with me. Let's go!

> (*A comforting* **BRITISH VOICE OVER.**)

> (*Shift.*)

VOICE-OVER. *Welcome to Starfighter.*
The small bridge seems to be devoid of any officers. Dust covers all of the instruments.
It appears as though things haven't been used for quite a while...

> Welcome to STARFIGHTER.
> The small bridge seems to be devoid of any officers. Dust covers all of the instruments.
> It appears as though things haven't been used for quite a while...

STARSINGER. Where are we?

LEGBA. Starfighter. It's cool.

/ So, what do you do for fun?

STARSINGER. Why is it cool?

What?

LEGBA. No, for fun! /

Before this I mean!

STARSINGER. / I'm just regular.

LEGBA. I never even knew something / like THIS could happen.

STARSINGER. What do you do?

> (**LEGBA [FEMALE]** *lines are now spoken in unison with* **LEGBA [MALE]**, *portrayed by* **MR. BUNGLE.**)

> **LEGBA** begins to float.

LEGBA (FEMALE & MALE). I'm in college.

STARSINGER. Ahhh, where?

LEGBA (FEMALE & MALE). Mass.

STARSINGER. Cool –

LEGBA (FEMALE & MALE). But I do lots of things.

I like to go out with friends, and to parties.

I go to the gym a lot.

STARSINGER. That's not fun, the gym!

LEGBA (FEMALE & MALE). Did you ever play sports?

STARSINGER. Yeah! Softball and soccer.

LEGBA (FEMALE & MALE). Total Jock!

STARSINGER. No!

In high school.

LEGBA (FEMALE & MALE). I had fun on my teams in high school, but wasn't good enough for college.

So the working out is to stay in shape.

STARSINGER. Are you in good shape?

LEGBA (FEMALE & MALE). Pretty good! What about you?

STARSINGER. Yeah.

LEGBA (FEMALE & MALE). Cool.

Do you have any pics on the net?

STARSINGER. No. I get shy. /

Do you?

LEGBA (FEMALE & MALE). I understand that.

Were you on any teams in college?

STARSINGER. No.

LEGBA (FEMALE & MALE). Same. I stopped in college.

Were the tryouts hard or did most people make it on the teams?

STARSINGER. Half and Half. I was good.

At my school.

(**LEGBA [FEMALE]** *fades out. Only* **LEGBA [MALE]** *remains.)*

LEGBA (MALE). Do you have a boyfriend?

STARSINGER. No.

LEGBA (MALE). My school was so small. They wanted people to go out for stuff.

The coach part of the tryout was a joke

(I don't either.)

We really did goof around.

STARSINGER. Nice.

LEGBA (MALE). The only serious part of the tryout was the part with the doctor they brought in.

And even that wasn't hard –

STARSINGER. A doctor?

LEGBA (MALE). – Just not a joke...

STARSINGER. To look you over?

LEGBA (MALE). Did you have that?

STARSINGER. No...

/ We did not have that.

LEGBA (MALE). / Yeah. It was fine.

It was just a checkup.

A little awkward at times, but no big deal.

STARSINGER. Awkward?

LEGBA (MALE). Yeah, they used a classroom for it, so I guess it kind of felt out of place.

(*Beat.*)

STARSINGER. ...I have to go soon...

LEGBA (MALE). Yeah, the school arranged for a doctor to come in one day after school and give the people trying out for teams a quick checkup.

STARSINGER. And that was odd?

LEGBA (MALE). I don't think it was odd.

STARSINGER. Because of the classroom?

LEGBA (MALE). Do you?

STARSINGER. No, I suppose not?

LEGBA (MALE). I just meant that it was out of place.

Studying math in a doctor's office would probably feel weird too...

Do you think that schools should make a point of bringing in a female doctor for girls and a male doctor for boys or do you think it doesn't matter?

STARSINGER. Well, most schools make a female be in the room, was it a / male?

LEGBA (MALE). No, we had a woman.

Did you get checkups in school for things other than sports?

STARSINGER. No!

Did YOU?

LEGBA (MALE). No, just the ones for sports.

If the doc is same-sex, do you think they should have to give you a gown to wear? / Or is it okay not to have a gown?

STARSINGER. Yes, I do.

Did you not have a gown??

LEGBA (MALE). No, no we didn't.

What would you let someone keep on under the gown at the beginning?

STARSINGER. ...Underwear?

LEGBA (MALE). Me too.

I'd go bra and panties either way.

STARSINGER. Did that happen to you?

LEGBA (MALE). Yeah, no gown.

STARSINGER. Were you okay?

LEGBA (MALE). Like I said, it was a little awkward, but yeah, it was okay.

STARSINGER.	**LEGBA (MALE).**
So you just thought it was odd?	I'm glad I wasn't at Starsinger School sitting in just my panties!
I'm not understanding?	

(LEGBA [MALE] giggles.)

I didn't like it, but, like, I was okay with it.

So, you want a girl to have her bra off the whole time gown or no gown?

STARSINGER. Hmmmmmm.

I should go...

LEGBA (MALE). I mean, you could say panties only with a gown, but bra and panties without to allow some modesty?

STARSINGER. I should go...

/ but nice talking to you!

LEGBA (MALE). Maybe we can chat again later? /

I like talking to you too.

STARSINGER. Maybe we can chat again later.

LEGBA (MALE). I like talking to you too.

Can you stay a couple more minutes?

STARSINGER. I have to go –

LEGBA (MALE). Would you include a breast exam or are you just thinking bra off to make it *easier* to listen to the heart, examine chest, etc?

STARSINGER. We'll have to talk later!

LEGBA (MALE). Sure. Let's meet in The Coat Closet?

STARSINGER. The Coat Closet, sure?

LEGBA (MALE). What time? Let's / meet at ten.

STARSINGER. Nice meeting you Jill!

LEGBA (MALE). Then we can tele / port.

STARSINGER. Teleport / where?

LEGBA (MALE). Do you think that if you were wearing say, like, overalls –

STARSINGER. Sorry –

LEGBA (MALE). With that weird back flap thing –

STARSINGER. I have to run –

See you…at ten!

    (Shift.)

> **STARSINGER** leaps into another dimension!

9PM: THE PARTY IN THE LIVING ROOM

(The party sounds are more distant, the chatter and the music muted, but still there.)

(The focus becomes The Puppet Bar.)

MR. BUNGLE. Mr. Bungle here.
Displacement... Momentum... Probability.

(Laughs.)

I know how many jelly beans there are in the jar because I *put them in the jar myself* and you really can't get angry if you're the one that purchases too many raffle tickets? You know the odds are more likely you'll end up missing that train, tearing that blouse, spilling coffee on your best shirt.

In the past everything was blamed on bad beef, dirty socks, the fear of the color yellow. Curiosity becomes a nuisance, pleasure becomes fear, strawberries become goldfish, still we continue to be excited when we find everything around us unrecognizable. This is what we've wished for. Why we are here. We don't worry about the future.

I'm really not the one of interest here...
When it's over I'll simply –
Leave the room.
Turn off my computer.
Close my eyes.
I'll pour myself a drink and open the window to feel the breeze.
It was cool that night, it felt good.

Mr. Bungle here.
Displacement... Momentum... Probability.

I know how many jelly beans there are in the jar because I *put them in the jar myself* and you really can't get angry if you're the one that purchases too many raffle tickets? You know the odds are more likely you'll end up missing that train, tearing that blouse, spilling coffee on your best shirt.

In the past everything was blamed on bad beef, dirty socks, the fear of the color yellow. Curiosity becomes a nuisance, pleasure becomes fear, strawberries become goldfish, still we continue to be excited when we find everything around us unrecognizable. This is what we've wished for. Why we are here. We don't worry about the future.

I'm really not the one of interest here...
When it's over I'll simply –
Leave the room.
Turn off my computer.
Close my eyes.
I'll pour myself a drink and open the window to feel the breeze.
It was cool that night, it felt good.

9:58PM: THE PARTY IN THE LIVING ROOM

JULIAN. Word of Starsinger's performance spread from the Master Bedroom to the Secluded Grove, from the MOOniversal Life Church all the way to Roger Ebert's House of Pudding. People came from every corner of LambdaMOO.

No one wanted to miss it for many of the reasons, or really for that one reason I told you at the beginning – it was shaping up to be a "you had to be there" sort of night.

PURPLE GUEST. *(Typing.) The crowd is gathering...if you squint your eyes you can see faces pressed against the inside of the windows on the hotels lining the Monopoly board, they are peering out – trying to see what's happening.*

JULIAN. It was a phenomenon in the making. She came back from Starfighter weirded out sure, but somehow invigorated. *Shinier.* I should have warned her not to teleport with people she just met.

> THE LIVING ROOM: It is very bright, open, and airy here, with large plate-glass windows looking southward over the pool to the gardens beyond. On the north wall, there is a rough stonework fireplace. There is a coffee table with a Monopoly board on it. The east and west walls are almost completely covered with large, well-stocked bookcases. There are two sets of couches, one clustered around the fireplace and one with a view out the windows. You see the Welcome Poster, a fireplace, the living room couch, Cockatoo, pinball machine, a large mirror, and The Birthday Machine.

(Shift.)

STARSINGER. – It was impossible to / to even understand what was happening –

> PURPLE GUEST is sleeping.

DR. BOMBAY. / Doctors?

STARSINGER. And I was like / sweating.

DR. BOMBAY. Gowns?

JUNIPER. *(Typing.) Juniper arrives fashionably early, yet another family trait he's borrowed from the generations of kings before him.*

STARSINGER. Dripping sweat –

JUNIPER. *He enjoys the certain level of agility –*

STARSINGER. – My heart, like pounding –

JUNIPER. *– That goes with being a squirrel and he takes the opportunity to climb up the stone face of the fireplace in The Living Room to watch over his fine feathered friends from above.*

STARSINGER. I even teleported!

DR. BOMBAY. Bravo!

STARSINGER. Then I'm not sure what happened?

DR. BOMBAY. I think he was –

STARSINGER. Jill. Her name was Jill.
    She was in / college?

DR. BOMBAY. / Uh-huh.

PURPLE GUEST. Has anyone been to The Hot Tub Room?

STARSINGER. Or I was confused?

PURPLE GUEST. Or the café that turns you French?

DR. BOMBAY. Petit-suisse!

PURPLE GUEST. Cream / Cheese!

JUNIPER. Bless you!

STARSINGER. Someone was confused.

JUNIPER. There's a bowling / alley –

PURPLE GUEST. Salt water.

JUNIPER. – Near the Cantina.

PURPLE GUEST. In the tubs.

DR. BOMBAY. Will Jill be at the show?

STARSINGER. Oh nononononononono!

PURPLE GUEST. I can't make your show.

DR. BOMBAY. Speaking of, everyone's here. /

PURPLE GUEST. I'm basically gone.

STARSINGER. / No way – /

DR. BOMBAY. / Yes – /

STARSINGER. (*Excited!*) / Stop it! /

PURPLE GUEST. Makes you feel like you're in
    space.
    The salt water.

LEGBA. It's also good for gargling.

DR. BOMBAY. Do you have your song?

STARSINGER. My song! Almost –

LEGBA. Hey, can I list someone as a pet reference?

DR. BOMBAY. Sure!

PURPLE GUEST. Later friends.

STARSINGER. I need to change! I'll be right
    back.

> (**STARSINGER** *turns out of the action again. During the following, until she
> comes back for her performance, we see her changing into her show dress in the
> shadows and primping...perhaps* **MR. BUNGLE** *helps her zip up the back of it.*)

LEGBA. It's...a very large pet. /
    I just need to make sure you understand what you're getting yourself into.

DR. BOMBAY. How large can it be? /
    What are / we talking here?

JUNIPER. I had a Great Dane...

LEGBA. Brontosaurus.

JUNIPER. Jelly. / Her name was...

JUNIPER's picking apples from the ceiling tree!

PURPLE GUEST flies around the room, looking everyone in the eyes.

LEGBA teleports in.

PURPLE GUEST leaps to another dimension.

(Singing softly to himself.)

JELLY-BEAN.

LEGBA. Or Tyrannosaurus or something. /
  BIG. / I need a HUGE pet.

DR. BOMBAY. You'll have to / build a new room –

LEGBA. I don't want like a dog or a cat or a
  fucking cow or anything.

STARSINGER is sleeping.

  I want a pet. And speaking as both a
  Haitian Witch AND a Doctor,
  I'd say a pet cow is 100 percent stupid.
  SO. I started thinking…
  Fuck fish and turtles and frogs.
  I want a dinosaur.
  And I definitely, definitely don't want a Pterodactyl because
  I hate shit that flies.
  So, then I'm like, ugh, which?
  B-Saurs? T-Rex?
  Then it was massively clear, clear on certain levels,
  clear that this is the culmination of my entire personal history – A Theme Park.
  I'm building A Theme Park.
  (But not like Jurassic-fucking-Park)
  But still, with Dinosaurs.

> *(**STARSINGER**'s music starts. There are lots of bars of intro music to it. Too many almost.)*

DR. BOMBAY. …I think she's about to begin.

> *(**STARSINGER** has emerged a star in a beautiful silky lounge singing dress. **MR. BUNGLE** appears…the light going on dimly in his puppet theater.)*

STARSINGER. Good evening –

> *(There is a smattering of hollers and applause.)*

A RAPE IN CYBERSPACE
By Julian Dibbell

STARSINGER. I wouldn't be here tonight if Dr. Bombay hadn't introduced me to this first number, here's to him.

> *(**STARSINGER** sings this as a slow, sexy torch song, keeping the tune of the original song, but adjusted to fit the lounge-like performance.)*

> *(Though the song is intercut with **JULIAN** reading from his article, the music does not stop when he speaks, but underscores his text. The music should help evoke that the night of this performance is the same night as the incident of which **JULIAN** is speaking.)*

(Other characters may be present taking in the performance or in the moment of the terrible act, but in front of their "computers.")

*(The projections hold when **STARSINGER** is singing and scroll when **JULIAN** speaks, mirroring what he says. The title of the article [the "A Rape in Cyberspace" projection] should remain fixed at the top during the entire scene so that the sections **JULIAN** reads scroll up into it and disappear. **STARSINGER** should have a really cool mic that makes her sound amazing, preferably with lots of reverb.)*

STARSINGER.

 LOOK FOR THE SILVER LINING
 WHENEVER A CLOUD APPEARS IN THE BLUE
 REMEMBER SOMEWHERE THE SUN IS SHINING
 AND SO THE RIGHT THING TO DO
 IS MAKE IT SHINE FOR YOU...

JULIAN. "They say he raped them that night. They say he did it with a cunning little doll, fashioned in their image and imbued with the power to make them do whatever he desired. They say that by manipulating the doll he forced them to have sex with him, and with each other, and to do horrible, brutal things to their own bodies..."

They say he raped them that night. They say he did it with a cunning little doll, fashioned in their image and imbued with the power to make them do whatever he desired. They say that by manipulating the doll he forced them to have sex with him, and with each other, and to do horrible, brutal things to their own bodies...

STARSINGER.

 A HEART FULL OF LOVE AND GLADNESS...
 WILL ALWAYS BANISH SADNESS AND
  STRIFE...

JULIAN. "The actors in the drama sat rather undramatically before computer screens the entire time, their only actions a spidery flitting of fingers across standard QWERTY keyboards. No bodies touched. Whatever physical interaction occurred consisted of a mingling of electronic signals sent from sites spread out between New York City and Sydney, Australia. Those signals met in LambdaMOO, certainly, just as the hideous clown and the living room party did, but what was LambdaMOO after all?"

The actors in the drama sat rather undramatically before computer screens the entire time, their only actions a spidery flitting of fingers across standard QWERTY keyboards. No bodies touched. Whatever physical interaction occurred consisted of a mingling of electronic signals sent from sites spread out between New York City and Sydney, Australia. Those signals met in LambdaMOO, certainly, just as the hideous clown and the living room party did, but what was LambdaMOO after all?

STARSINGER.

 SO ALWAYS LOOK FOR THE SILVER
  LINING
 AND TRY TO FIND THE SUNNY SIDE OF LIFE.

JULIAN. *"LambdaMOOers are allowed a broad freedom to create – they can describe their characters any way they like, they can make rooms of their own and decorate them to taste, and they can build new objects almost at will. The combination of all this busy user activity with the hard physics of the database can certainly induce a lucid illusion of presence – but when all is said and done the only thing you really see when you visit LambdaMOO is a kind of slow-crawling script, lines of dialogue and stage direction creeping steadily up your computer screen."

*LambdaMOOers are allowed a broad freedom to create – they can describe their characters any way they like, they can make rooms of their own and decorate them to taste, and they can build new objects almost at will. The combination of all this busy user activity with the hard physics of the database can certainly induce a lucid illusion of presence – but when all is said and done the only thing you really see when you visit LambdaMOO is a kind of slow-crawling script, lines of dialogue and stage direction creeping steadily up your computer screen.

(Simultaneously, the following. At the discretion of the production certain words and phrases should stand out over others.)

STARSINGER.

LOOK FOR THE SILVER
  LINING
WHENEVER A CLOUD
  APPEARS IN THE
  BLUE
REMEMBER
  SOMEWHERE THE
  SUN IS SHINING
AND SO THE RIGHT
  THING TO DO
IS MAKE IT SHINE FOR
  YOU...

A HEART FULL OF LOVE
  AND GLADNESS...
WILL ALWAYS BANISH
  SADNESS AND
  STRIFE...
SO ALWAYS LOOK FOR
THE SILVER LINING
AND TRY TO FIND THE
SUNNY SIDE OF LIFE

JULIAN
"They tell us that he commenced his assault entirely unprovoked, at or about 10 p.m. Pacific Standard Time. That he began by using his Voodoo doll to force one of the room's occupants to sexually service him in a variety of more or less conventional ways. That this victim was Legba, a Haitian trickster spirit of indeterminate gender, brown skinned and wearing an expensive pearl gray suit, top hat, and dark glasses. He turned his attentions now to Starsinger, a rather pointedly nondescript female character, tall, stout, and brown haired, forcing her into unwanted liaisons with other individuals present in the room, among them Legbo and Juniper (the squirrel).

They tell us that he commenced his assault entirely unprovoked, at or about 10 p.m. Pacific Standard Time. That he began by using his Voodoo doll to force one of the room's occupants to sexually service him in a variety of more or less conventional ways. That this victim was legba, a Haitian trickster spirit of indeterminate gender, brown skinned and wearing an expensive pearl gray suit, top hat, and dark glasses. He turned his attentions now to Starsinger, a rather pointedly nondescript female character, tall, stout, and brown haired, forcing her into unwanted liaisons with other individuals present in the room, among them Legba, and Juniper (the squirrel).

(JULIAN and STARSINGER become engaged in a strange duet of back and forth [Not to imply JULIAN sings, he does not.] The energy between them should rise throughout the following, so by the end, it's a standoff. The arrangement of the song and the intention of STARSINGER's singing should change – become impassioned in a new way – as she becomes aware of what JULIAN is saying.)

STARSINGER.
  ...AND TRY TO FIND THE SUNNY SIDE OF LIFE...

JULIAN. "That his actions grew progressively violent."

> That his actions grew progressively violent.

STARSINGER.
  JUST...
  LOOK FOR THE SILVER LINING –

JULIAN. "That he made Legba eat his/her own pubic hair."

> That he made Legba eat his/her own pubic hair.

STARSINGER.
  WHENEVER A CLOUD APPEARS IN THE BLUE –

JULIAN. "That he caused Starsinger to violate herself with a piece of kitchen cutlery."

> That he caused Starsinger to violate herself with a piece of kitchen cutlery.

STARSINGER.
  REMEMBER SOMEWHERE THE SUN IS SHINING –

JULIAN. "That his distant laughter echoed evilly in the living room with every successive outrage."

> That his distant laughter echoed evilly in the living room with every successive outrage.

STARSINGER.
  AND SO THE RIGHT THING TO DO –
  IS MAKE IT SHINE FOR YOU!!

(Her song has ended. A few moments of silence as they take each other in.)

JULIAN. "He had committed a MOO crime... LamdaMOO would just have to grow up and solve its problems on its own..."

> He had committed a MOO crime... LamdaMOO would just have to grow up and solve its problems on its own...
>
> (Excerpt *Village Voice*, 1993)

(They are mid-conversation.)

JULIAN. This is part of our common story. Human nature. If you take part in something, anything, long enough – things...happen.

CHUCK PETAL. Okay Julian, thanks for that, that blistering insight.

    (To **JOHN.***)* Before we go, talk about Bill Gates. Who we all know.

JOHN. Well, I wanted to send an e-mail to Bill Gates –

CHUCK PETAL. Now, how did you get his e-mail number?

JOHN. His "address." It was really easy. I just called up a guy I knew that was in the computer biz, and he had it. So, I sent Bill a message – it helped that I was writing a story for *The New Yorker* – and he responded in –

    (Dramatic and incredulous.)

    – eighteen minutes.

CHUCK PETAL. *(Deeply, deeply impressed.)* Eighteen minutes!

JOHN. Eighteen minutes.

CHUCK PETAL. Imagine! So, he must have been at his computer or something? Because he didn't know you would be

    doing that, calling –

JOHN. E-mailing.

CHUCK PETAL. E-mailing.

JOHN. Correct.

CHUCK PETAL. How about that. Eighteen minutes.

JOHN. Eighteen minutes.

CHUCK PETAL. Eighteen minutes.

JULIAN. *(Dryly.)* Eighteen minutes.

JOHN. Then, we e-mailed.

CHUCK PETAL. You send a message and he responds. He sends a message and you respond. You send a message and he responds. He sends –

JOHN. I mean, he must have been there, / been in front of his computer.

CHUCK PETAL. He must have just been there, in front of his computer.

JOHN. He might have even had something that was telling him he was getting new mail. An indicator of some sort. It was like... I was shocked.

CHUCK PETAL. It shocked you.

JOHN. Electrically shocked when I saw his e-mail. Literally blown back away from my computer screen.

CHUCK PETAL. His response was so fast.

JOHN. So then, I started interviewing him through e-mail. Back and forth –

CHUCK PETAL. And back and forth.

JOHN. And it was actually a really interesting way to conduct an interview.

CHUCK PETAL. You *learned* things from him.

JOHN. He started to open up, divulge different parts of himself to me through words. But then...

CHUCK PETAL. Yes?

JOHN. After the interview was over –

> *(Falters.)*

– and the piece came out –

> *(Getting upset.)*

– he stopped e-mailing me.

CHUCK PETAL. Because the interview was over.

JOHN. Whatever.

CHUCK PETAL. The article was out.

JOHN. I was like?? Thanks. Bill.

CHUCK PETAL. You were done.

JOHN. Gates.

CHUCK PETAL. The article was over.

JOHN. I guess I didn't really expect him to keep it up, but??

JULIAN. But that's normal though.

JOHN. Did you know he was unpopular in high school?

JULIAN. You had engaged him for a specific purpose.

JOHN. That he believes in failure as a tool –

JULIAN. See, this is all going to get very, very complicated. It already is. Expectations – like the ones you had, the friendship you thought you'd formed –

JOHN. Eighteen minutes.

JULIAN. Yes, that's, ah, quick.

CHUCK PETAL. But – you weren't done with Bill Gates.

JOHN. I make it out to Seattle sometimes...

CHUCK PETAL. You thought he'd invite you to "a party in Buffalo."

JOHN. Did you know he loves dogs?

CHUCK PETAL. You wanted him to invite you and your wife over for a barbecue.

JOHN. That he's fond of sitting and staring at large bodies of water?

JULIAN. This is exactly what's so interesting –

JOHN. That it calms him?

JULIAN. – The social phenomenon, the stigma attached to creating – or thinking you are creating – a relationship that, in fact, is not there.

CHUCK PETAL. Bill Gates was not there.

JULIAN. No, of course he was there. But to him, this is just another method of getting work done. Simply easier than picking up the phone. And to you, it was more intimate than that.

JOHN. You don't just share this sort of information –

JULIAN. Yes. Yes you do.

> *(Beat.)*

CHUCK PETAL. And I think we'll rest it there for the night. Be sure to hold tight to those in "real life" because it looks like we're in for a wild ride if "Internet" catches on. I want to thank Julian – Dr. Bombay – for sharing his insight, for reminding all of us of the Mr. Bungles out there. And to our man from *The New Yorker*, "Bambi."

And – hey – Bill Gates, maybe I'll be e-mailing you around.

I AM REQUESTING THAT MR. BUNGLE BE TOADED

(**JUNIPER, STARSINGER,** and **LEGBA** *each have something from RL with them.*)

(**JUNIPER** *a drink.* **STARSINGER** *a bag of her favorite chips.* **LEGBA** *a lollipop and a Walkman, etc.*)

(**MR. BUNGLE** *is doing something small and domestic – completing his laundry, doing a puzzle, reading a book – he's lightly present, but not really.*)

(*The projections* for The Living Room run in all directions, sizes, fonts, the system has broken down...something is amiss...*)

LEGBA. *(Typing.) Legba's top hat has been knocked*
/ across the room...

STARSINGER. *(Typing.) A microphone lies on*
the floor,
then disappears completely / into the
Persian rug...

JUNIPER. *(Typing.) Juniper is unsure where*
to look, unable to help his friends, he's
suddenly no longer...thirsty...

LEGBA. *(Typing.) The Living Room has*
grown old,
grown cold,
there are cobwebs across the windows
a thin layer of dust hangs in the air like
one of Saturn's rings.

STARSINGER. *(Typing.) The Monopoly board*
is abandoned,
mid-game on the coffee table.
Someone is looting Marvin Gardens.

JUNIPER. *(Typing.) Through the curtains a*
few bright indicators
tell us that day is out there. Though this was
before Juniper's hangover was so consuming
/ he could not tell if something was wrong or right
happy or sad.

LEGBA. *(Typing.) Before Legba had grown quiet,*
hanging back by the bookshelf surrounded
by books that teach underwater navigation,
that show how to store Methadone.

(**Scrolling and repeated...*)
THE LIVING ROOM: It is very bright, open, and airy here, with large plate-glass windows looking southward over the pool to the gardens beyond. On the north wall, there is a rough stonework fireplace. There is a coffee table with a Monopoly board on it. The east and west walls are almost completely covered with large, well-stocked bookcases. There are two sets of couches, one clustered around the fireplace and one with a view out the windows. You see the Welcome Poster, a fireplace, the living room couch, Cockatoo, pinball machine, a large mirror, and The Birthday Machine.

(*Shift.* **LEGBA** *does something swift and violent – throws a table, kicks her chair over.*)

(*She puts her Walkman on and hits play. We can hear the beginning of a song in the style of 4 Non Blondes' hit song from 1993, "What's Up."* After a few moments the song may become a bigger presence, growing louder and louder, allowing* **LEGBA** *a moment of angst and unplaced anger.*)

(**JUNIPER, STARSINGER**, *and* **LEGBA** *may move to assume the positions from the Chuck Petal scene.*)

(*They now talk to each other as if they were on a talk show, like Chuck Petal. And even though they are in their own worlds, in one reality having internal thoughts, the conversation flows as if on a show in the same conversation.*)

STARSINGER. (*Just reporting the facts.*) I entered through The Coat Closet. I prepared. I sang my song. I didn't even ask what The Birthday Machine was, it was just there and that was fine. I was like, no, no, the Dutch are the only ones that are supposed to eat cheese. Then she was like something about Hibiscus and I was like: *Evolution.* I read that, some magazine, or something. The Dutch, you know?

JUNIPER. This is Frog and Toad all over again.

LEGBA. I was...
Just there / for the *concert.*

JUNIPER. How did we get here?

STARSINGER. I came through / The Coat Closet.

JUNIPER. I just came through The Coat Closet.

STARSINGER. It's exactly what my Aunt Rita used to say. If there's a man, and that man has a puppet – sock puppet, strings, Sharpie on hand, whatever, seriously, if that man has a puppet then just like, beware.

LEGBA. *Fuck...him.*

STARSINGER. Aunt Rita would say, hell, we'll look back on this and laugh –

LEGBA. I was me, I was me, then I was hitting, I was smashing the table, I tore off the Return key, I spat at the screen. Then it wasn't me.

STARSINGER. That's what's so wild! He could be anyone!

JUNIPER. A dog, it could / be a dog.

LEGBA. This is insane.

(**LEGBA** *stands up as if to leave.*)

STARSINGER. (*Under her breath.*) I wouldn't even have been here tonight if Dr. Bombay hadn't introduced me to that first number.

JUNIPER. Sorry to –
Sorry / to –

(**LEGBA** *sits back down.*)

LEGBA. I am requesting that Mr. Bungle be Toaded.

JUNIPER. Toaded, yes, Frog and Toad, the books, the Frog and Toad books have had tremendous influence over me as both a copywriter and as, well...and here's what I

---

*A license to produce *If You Can Get to Buffalo* does not include a performance license for any third-party or copyrighted music. Licensees should create an original composition or use music in the public domain. For further information, please see Music Use Note on page 3.

think: when you look at it, Toads are fairly odd creatures. And there's a reason they're not commonly viewed say as a mascot or a lead in a film or even like the star of a really good metaphor. With, with, haha, with the exception to THIS being:

Frog and Toad.

Why I bring this up is to draw a parallel that perhaps you,

we,

you,

we,

you

I have not thought of yet. Not in *Frog and Toad are Friends*, not in *Frog and Toad Together*, but in *DAYS with Frog and Toad* there's a misunderstanding of sorts and Toad is upset because Frog – wait for it – Frog:

"wants to be alone."

And he, *Toad*, he thinks, assumes, it's his fault. But it's not.

Frog wants to be alone because – wait for it – he's, *he's happy.*

He wants to sit there,

alone on that rock

in the middle of that river,

he wants to sit there

and think about "how fine everything is."

> *(Beat.)*

> *(**STARSINGER** starts laughing. She eats a chip.)*

LEGBA. I am requesting that Mr. Bungle be Toaded.

JUNIPER. Toading Mr. Bungle. Sure – but he'd probably love that!

STARSINGER. All I'm saying is that I *was* singing.

But then I wasn't.

But I wasn't doing. It. Things. That wasn't me?

LEGBA. Is anyone else physically sick over this?

STARSINGER. It was like the *best part* of the song.

JUNIPER. I am not ashamed to say I am confused.

LEGBA. It was / confusing.

JUNIPER. ...Scrolling so fast. Was it / an org–

LEGBA. It was terrorism.

STARSINGER. Where was Dr. Bombay?

> *(**LEGBA** stands up as if to leave.)*

I wouldn't even have been here tonight if Dr. Bombay hadn't introduced me to that first number.

> *(**LEGBA** sits back down.)*

LEGBA. I am requesting that Mr. Bungle be Toaded.

STARSINGER. Toaded?

LEGBA. To Toad someone is to, well, delete them.

STARSINGER. *(Questioning.)* Toading him / is –

LEGBA. To Toad someone is to, well, delete them.

JUNIPER. History erased.

STARSINGER. So, Mr. Bungle would not
    be the name –

LEGBA. Of any char / acter.

JUNIPER. Of any character.

> (**LEGBA** *stands up as if to leave. Sits back down.*)

LEGBA. I am requesting that Mr. Bungle be Toaded.

STARSINGER. *(Oh, how disappointing.)*
    There will now be rules?
    Yeah. Let's do it.

> **LEGBA** nods solemnly.

*(Typing.) Legba seems lost without her
Top Hat and Starsinger goes to retrieve it. She steps over The Birthday Machine which is
laying, er, lying on its side near the giant stuffed polar bear.*

> (**LEGBA** *stands up as if to leave. Sits back down.*)

JUNIPER. *(Typing.) Unlike most squirrels, Juniper fully supports his Living Room friends
    and –*

LEGBA. These actions will not be tolerated –

JUNIPER. *(Typing.) – And understands that these actions will not be tolerated.*

LEGBA. I am requesting that Mr. Bungle be Toaded.

STARSINGER. *(Typing.) She returns the hat to Legba in a show of solidarity.*

JUNIPER. Let's Toad the bastard.
    (Typing.) He drinks the last of his drink.
    He looks in the glass.
    He realizes it's empty.
    He goes to get another.

> (**JUNIPER** *exits.*)

LEGBA. Let's Toad the bastard.

> (**LEGBA** *is distraught, but satisfied.*)

> (**MR. BUNGLE** *is magically done folding his laundry at precisely this time.*)

> (*He gathers it all in his arms.*)

> (**MR. BUNGLE** *exits.*)

> (**STARSINGER** *keeps trying to
> teleport out by reprising
> whatever action she attempted
> during the Dining Room scene.*)

> You can't go that way.

> (**STARSINGER** *tries the command
> again.*)

> You can't go that way.

> (**STARSINGER** *tries again.*)

> You can't go that way.

> (**STARSINGER** *tries again.*)

> (**STARSINGER** *exits.*)

> **STARSINGER** teleports out.

> (*Shift.*)

JULIAN. I was telling my friend Shelly about this whole thing. How it went down, about the article I was bound to write, how it was like perfect timing – Bungle coming when so many people would be in The Living Room – when there was such a fever about Starsinger's "performance."
I told Shelly about how she'd been shy and nervous...but she was just starting to feel comfortable. I told her about how she didn't like pickled okra, but that she *did* like pickles. *And*, she liked me.

（*Smiles.*）

I am so stupid.
I was looking forward to these long talks in The Living Room and strolls around the Mansion. There was this room I really wanted to show her. It was back through The Dining Room, out past the Kitchen Patio, across the Lilypad Lawn, back through the garage and up the stairs. I didn't create it, just stumbled upon it; it's called "La Cantina de los Puertos del Mundo."
It's a room where anything was possible.
You *never* spill like coffee, or shit on your clothes.
No one *ever* called you an asshole
and you were *always* under the assumption, because this is what the room told you, that people were listening to you.
That you were interesting.
In this room you always got the girl.

（*Beat.*）

I wasn't there that night. I'd set Starsinger up for this whole show and then...and this isn't even a good excuse...I just lost track of *time*...was doing something else...and then, I was like *shit*. It's 10:30. *Ugh*.

（**LEGBA** *hands him a pie box, then exits.*）

Thanks.
I eat pie when I'm depressed.

（*Bashfully.*）

A lot of pie sometimes.
Mainly cherry...
I prefer Cherry to...
Say...Key Lime.

JOHN (FROM THE NEW YORKER) JOINS "BILL GATES" IN "SEATTLE" FOR A BARBECUE

(**JOHN** and **"BILL GATES"** [**WIFE**] are barbecuing.)

(Hyper-natural outdoor sounds: birds, children playing, sprinklers.)

JOHN. Hi...

Bill Gates.

BILL GATES. (She speaks fairly stilted, a first-timer herself.) Thank you for seeing me on your busy trip to Seattle.

JOHN. No prob.

That's what old friends do.

BILL GATES. Right-o.

JOHN. (Attempting to be breezy and cool.) Right-o Chuck-o.

Dig your glasses.

BILL GATES. I wasn't / sure...

JOHN. They pop.

BILL GATES. About the frames.

JOHN. The frames pop.

BILL GATES. Do you like the frames?

JOHN. The frames pop.

So, whatcha got on the grill there?

BILL GATES. MEAT.

JOHN. Ah, meat...

It's hard.

/ To be a kid with glasses.

BILL GATES. It was hard.

JOHN. You must have had to deal with a lot.

BILL GATES. They called me things like...

Dork. Fuck.

JOHN. I don't know if you saw me? /

But I was recently on –

BILL GATES. / Dork-Fuck.

JOHN. The Chuck / Petal Show.

BILL GATES. After I saw you on Chuck Petal I realized...

I *had* to see you.

JOHN. *Oh Bill.*

(Laughing.)

JOHN. I was so...

embarrassed by that.

BILL GATES. You're so in touch with your emotions.

It...

(Whispering.)

YOU –

Moved me.

JOHN. I hope I'm not interrupting your / work.

BILL GATES. The sausage is almost –

JOHN. Your important computer work.

BILL GATES. My computer work can wait.

JOHN. Oh Bill.

Little hot out here, are you hot Bill...?

(Shift.)

(Everyone has left the stage. All is quiet.)

(The projections disappear, there are none.)

*(**CHUCK PETAL** enters, cautiously, and takes a seat at the table in front of a keyboard.)*

(An old-school modem is heard dialing up.)

CHUCK PETAL. *(Typing.)* I really want to meet you...see you face to face.

(He's very pleased with himself.)

There's this party in Buffalo, it's going to be off the hook.

It's at someone named Oscar's house.

A huge place with this hot tub that's FULL of champagne.

His parents are gone and we're taking the place over.

They're gone like...ALLLLLLLLL weekend.

It's going to be fucked up if you get what I mean –

know what I'm saying –

You know?

Can you come?

If you can get to Buffalo I swear I'll be personally responsible for your good time.

I know how to treat people right.

You don't even understand how hard we rock it in Buffalo.

See you there?

*(**CHUCK** type/talks this last question, "See you there?" then he kinda grimace-cringe-smiles in anticipation and hits Send.)*

End of Play

Look For The Silver Lining

Lyrics: Bud DeSylva
Music: Jerome Kern

www.ingramcontent.com/pod-product-compliance
Lightning Source LLC
Chambersburg PA
CBHW082055090726

47909CB00010B/3048